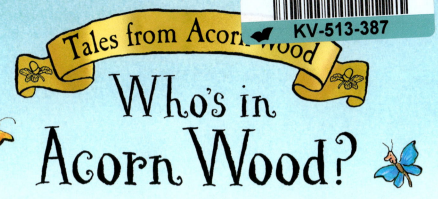

Tales from Acorn Wood

Who's in Acorn Wood?

JULIA DONALDSON ✻ AXEL SCHEFFLER

This Tales from Acorn Wood book belongs to

....

I celebrated World Book Day® 2025 with this gift from
my local bookseller and Macmillan Children's Books

WORLD BOOK DAY®

World Book Day's mission is to offer every child and young person the opportunity
to read and love books by giving you the chance to have a book of your own.
To find out more, and for fun activities including video stories, audiobooks
and book recommendations, visit worldbookday.com
World Book Day® is a charity sponsored by National Book Tokens.

The animals of Acorn Wood
have found their picnic tea.

The cups and plates are on the rug.
How many can you see?

Where is Fox's missing sock?
What's on Mouse's head?

Can you see a spider dangling from a thread?

Badger's band is playing.
Can you spot Hare's cello?

Can you see a bright blue flag,
a green one and a yellow?

Can you spot the slippers on Squirrel's bedside mat?

Who's outside her window with
a carrot, scarf and hat?

It's Frog's day out, with all his friends.
They love the sea and sand.

Can you find a fishbone?
What's in Hedgehog's hand?

Mole has asked his friends to tea.
Can you count them all?

Can you see his milk jug,
and the pictures on his wall?

The animals of Acorn Wood
are at the Acorn Fair.

Can you point to Dormouse, Badger, Owl and Bear?

Welcome to Acorn Wood!

CELEBRATING 25 YEARS

There are lots of lift-the-flap stories to discover:

Fox's Socks
JULIA DONALDSON · AXEL SCHEFFLER

Rabbit's Nap
JULIA DONALDSON · AXEL SCHEFFLER

Postman Bear
JULIA DONALDSON · AXEL SCHEFFLER

Hide-and-Seek Pig
JULIA DONALDSON · AXEL SCHEFFLER

Cat's Cookbook
JULIA DONALDSON · AXEL SCHEFFLER

Squirrel's Snowman
JULIA DONALDSON · AXEL SCHEFFLER

Mole's Spectacles
JULIA DONALDSON · AXEL SCHEFFLER

Badger's Band
JULIA DONALDSON · AXEL SCHEFFLER

Dormouse Has a Cold
JULIA DONALDSON · AXEL SCHEFFLER

Frog's Day Out
JULIA DONALDSON · AXEL SCHEFFLER

Coming Soon
Hare's New Dress